I Can, We Can

by Don L. Curry

SCHOLASTIC INC.

New York   Toronto   London   Auckland   Sydney
Mexico City   New Delhi   Hong Kong   Buenos Aires

I can look.

We can look.

I can hop.

We can hop.

I can ride.

We can ride.

I can play.

We can play.

Copyright © 2002 by Scholastic Inc.
All rights reserved. Published by Scholastic Inc.
Printed in the U.S.A.

ISBN 0-439-45557-X

20 19 18 17 16   40   13 14 15 16